HONEYCUTT'S
TRAVELING RODEO

AND

GENUINE OLD FASHIONED
MEDICINE SHOW

by

John Longbottom

RoseDog ❖ Books
PITTSBURGH, PENNSYLVANIA 15238

RoseDog Books
585 Alpha Drive, Suite 103
Pittsburgh, PA 15238
Visit our website at *www.rosedogbookstore.com*

ISBN: 978-1-6470-2119-1
eISBN: 978-1-6470-2138-2

To Mary

"The world is best viewed through the ears of a horse."

Author unknown.

HONEYCUTT'S
TRAVELING RODEO

AND

GENUINE OLD FASHIONED
MEDICINE SHOW

THE CREW

The cross-eyed clown and the midget, the one with the crooked grin, sat in the bed of a pick-up truck smoking cheap cigars and concocting clues for crossword puzzles just to while away the hours. Now, before all the Little People and the P. C. police start raising a ruckus, writing letters and carrying signs protesting the use of derogatory nomenclature, let me just explain that this particular midget vehemently refused to be called a dwarf.

"Dwarfs are irregular, disproportionate. My body is perfectly proportioned, except for one minor detail. I'm just small, that's all. Therefore, I'm a midget, not a dwarf," he would claim if anyone dared to call him the "d" word, which Joe the Indian frequently did.

Just then, right on cue, Joe the Indian came running past, his hands over his ears. It ain't easy to run with your hands over your ears. Somewhere there must be some fancy formula which explains why physics react with the anatomy causing imbalance. It is no easy task to run over rough terrain with your hands not over your ears, even when you're sober, but Joe was running like a drunk, and like a drunk, he kept falling over. You see, Joe the Indian just acted drunk 'cos he figured most people out west expected an Indian to be drunk, but truth be told, he hadn't touched a drop since Carter had been elected, except for one minor detail.

Joe fell once more into the ditch beside the road and let out a sound somewhere between a howl and a groan.

"What's up, Redskin, Custer's ghost coming to get ya?" The midget called out through his crooked smile.

A bare fist slowly arose out of the ditch and flashed the midget half a peace sign then, just as slowly, descended back out of sight accompanied by another dubious moan.

Those two just never got along, and some suspected it was the cause of the crooked smile. The midget's name was known to few, so to most he was just "midget." It all started 'cos Joe insisted on calling the midget a dwarf, and when he wouldn't stop, the midget started calling Joe, "Redskin." Or maybe it was the other way around; no one really knew. It wasn't that Joe the Indian was all that P. C. No sir, far from it. He could be just as offensive as the rest of us and playing drunk helped him get away with it: mostly. No, because of his heritage, he was sensitive about name calling and racially offensive epithets. He had read that Little People, across the board, preferred to be called either dwarfs or Little People. Consequently, he insisted on calling the midget "dwarf" out of respect. As he didn't know the midget's real name, "dwarf "it was.

"You should stand with your people and honor them," Joe the Indian said.

"They ain't my people," retorted the midget.

A bottomless argument ensued, and the rest is history.

Just another day at Honeycutt's Traveling Rodeo and Genuine Old Fashioned Medicine Show. No one knew who Honeycutt was or if he'd ever been. The whole ramshackle operation was run by the Sisters of Aberdeen. Or was it Abilene? No one really knew, not even the twins.

Yup, they were twins, and identical except for one minor detail: Abigail was four-foot-ten, and Zelda was six-foot-four whenever she stood erect, which wasn't very often, so everyone called her Stoop. In another world, at another time, she could have been a model, but those particular stars never shone over Zelda; she was destined to stoop forever but not to conquer.

A screech, a moan, and several cuss words cut through the peace of the afternoon. The reason for Indian Joe's hands-over-ears-running became apparent. Windows slammed shut, doors crashed closed, the cross-eyed clown and the midget moved inside, and Indian Joe almost wet himself scrambling to get out of the ditch into which he had fallen.

J.D. had gotten his fiddle out of hock and was practicing again. J.D. was one of those gifted people who could play any instrument he touched. And he played them well. Not just a few notes here and there for show. He was accomplished on them all, with one minor exception. The fiddle. He could not fathom the fiddle. He was out of his depth, and it irked him to no end. And, like abuse, that irk was passed on to the innocents around him. He would practice and practice and drive the others half mad with his frustrated curses at the spine-wrenching screeching of an inaccurate bow drawn across unforgiving strings. The only respite the others got was when J.D.'s frustrations peaked, or he ran out of money and would hock his cursed violin. As close as he had come, he could never smash up an instrument, even an uncooperative fiddle. He wasn't stupid either and soon cottoned on to the others trying to lure him into card games so that he would go broke faster and head for the pawn shop sooner. When he wasn't trying to play the fiddle, he was a gentle soul with a mischievous grin that belied the devilment within. J.D. faced life with the slightly sideways stance of a true musician. He had a twisted sense of humor, which could turn quite wicked, as if a wand were waved, when someone crossed him or complained about his lack of violinic virtuosity.

He was mildly famous amongst the crew of the Show. If you ask, no one will tell. The motto and unspoken rule of the whole operation was, "Ask no questions," but if you dig deep enough and apply just the right amount of liquid tongue loosener, you'll find that J.D. had a slight difference of opinion with the NAACP. He was wearing black-face and playing banjo at one of his shows claiming it was an authentic reenactment of a minstrel show. J.D. was a light-skinned African American. Not only was his pigmentation light, but his features were more Caucasian than black, and someone in the audience thought him white and took offence.

J.D. tried to laugh it off.

"Don't you see the irony?" he asked. "A black man wearing black face. You just can't get more absurd," he entreated. "Well, on second thought, I guess you could because I am now being persecuted."

Indian Joe had the devil of a time to talk him out of showing up at the hearing wearing clown's white face.

"I don't think they'll quite see it as a joke, J.D."

'Course it didn't help his case none that the initials J.D. stood for Jeffrey David. Even though his last name was Williams, it was close enough to a certain Confederate Colonel's name to cause concern for those for whom the world of nuance and subtlety was unexplored territory. J.D.'s father, although not a banjo strummer, was into irony, too, and his ancestors did trace back to that particular southern plantation.

"J.D., put that damn thing away afore someone gets killed."

Abigail, the shorter and older of the two sisters, came stomping around the corner.

"Ya cain't kill anyone with music, Miss Abbie," J.D. replied. "It's the food of love, according to Shakespeare."

"That ain't music, and it'll be the Winchester doing the killing not that infernal fiddle."

Abigail cranked the lever on the rifle just to make the point. That and one look at her face was all it took for J.D. to reluctantly and tenderly put the violin back in its case.

In spite of her small size, and gun or no gun, Miss Abbie was a force to be reckoned with. She had once deftly shot off the tip of the upraised middle finger of a rejected would-be suitor who was shouting derogatory comments about Abbie's presumed sexuality. As a shooter, she was up there with the best, both target and fancy trick shooting. As a horse rider and handler, she was a natural; in the saddle or bareback, both roping and barrel riding or just plain old wrangling, it didn't matter, Abigail's body and mind would become one with the horse. Sometimes, watching her ride, the midget could barely tell where Abbie ended, and the horse began. There are those that are better at both riding and shooting, but where Abbie shone was as the ramrod. As the boss and leader of this crew of mismatched souls, she stood head and shoulders above all the other wranglers, shooters, and cowboys.

Her face could be hard, as it was when she told J.D. to shut up, or gentle, depending on both her mood and yours, and of course, the lighting. Abigail's looks were on the cusp of beauty. With her short-cropped, gamine style hair, she was more than handsome but less than beautiful. Growing up, Abbie had always been called a tomboy; it didn't bother her then, it didn't bother her now. She was just Abbie, and Abbie was basically just happy as the co-owner of Honeycutt's Traveling Rodeo and Genuine Old Fashioned Medicine Show.

"Come on guys, get a move on."

Abbie's face was set in that "don't mess with me look," and with the rifle in hand as an added incentive, everyone jumped.

"The truck's finally fixed, and we can get this show on the road. We have to be in Clarinda by nightfall."

MAGDA

3:23 AM.

The cross-eyed clown turned and looked at the ubiquitous motel clock.

3:24 AM.

The night was so quiet and the clock so old that the clown could hear the numbers turn as the minutes flipped by. He should get going, back to his own trailer before the rest of the crew that awoke with the roosters started their own daily routines. With a quick look of longing at the woman sleeping soundly next to him, he gently slipped out of the bed, grabbed his clothes, dressed, and as quietly as possible tried to slip out of the motel room. There wasn't much danger of the woman waking up; they'd both had a skin full of booze the night before, and she had finally and thankfully passed out a couple of hours earlier.

• • • • •

The sisters who ran Honeycutt's Traveling Rodeo and Genuine Old Fashioned Medicine Show frowned on the crew fraternizing with the locals, especially the customers.

"You don't fish off company piers," proclaimed Zelda at the company meeting held a few weeks ago. She was the younger and taller of the twins.

"Vot, ve can no more fish?" cried Magda, the East European acrobat who had a problem with English comprehension.

She was ignored, as usual.

"Ain't that fishing thing about employees bangin' employees?" asked Spoke, one of the cowboys. "An' anyway, how y'all gonna enforce that? You gonna geld us all?"

"Nope. Next best thing, we'll take it out your wages," replied Zelda with a triumphant smirk.

That last comment caused a general ruckus with a chorus of, "That ain't fair." And, "You cain't do that, Stoop."

"Actually, we can. Remember that contract you signed when you first came on board?" Zelda held up a printed sheet of paper. There was an even louder chorus of discontent. Some rose to their feet, their fists in the air; others just shook their heads, and a couple just sat there and smiled.

They were all silenced by the crack of a bullwhip as Abbie moved into view.

"Y'all settle down now, ya hear?" and she glared at a couple of the more vocal of the protesters.

"Come on. Sit on back down. What we're trying to say is y'all got to be careful. We don't want to get a bad reputation, and we can't afford a repeat of what just happened a few weeks ago,"

Abigail avoided looking at Magda, but a few of the others looked very accusingly at her.

"Fault was not mine. Vy you always me blaming?" said Magda in her deep assertive voice.

The fault, indeed, was not Magda's. At some point during her act, Magda always invited a female member of the audience to help her out. It was a crowd pleaser, especially if she chose a pretty young woman. Magda was neither a sexist nor a lesbian, it was just the way showbusiness worked, and showbusiness is sexist. The men in the audience liked ogling a "purtty young thang," and most of the women could identify with her, especially if she were shy and nervous. A few weeks back, Magda asked for a volunteer, as usual. She had her eye on a young farmer's wife, there with her two kids and what looked to be their grandparents. Just as the woman was making her way towards the ring, she was roughly pushed aside by a rather brawny, black leather, and multi-colored ink clad woman who strode purposefully out to Magda and offered her services. The only sign that Magda was uncomfortable was in her eyes, and the audience was too far away to see their real concern. Like the seasoned veteran that she was, Magda carried on with the show.

The tattooed lady had been drinking; Magda could smell it on her breath as she aggressively pushed up close to Magda's body. A couple of times, Magda felt the other woman's hands brush across both her breasts and her lower abdomen. The crowd was getting uncomfortable, she could sense it and hear the growing number of murmurs as they, too, grew unsettled. After the leather lady planted a sloppy, beer tainted kiss on Magda's cheek, the performer, with perhaps more force than she intended, pushed the amorous woman away. Taken by surprise the woman turned; Magda's pushing hand slipped onto the leather clad breast of the woman who tripped over her own drink impaired feet and fell into a pile of horse shit left by the previous act. The crowd thought this was hilarious and exploded with laughter, now almost certain that this was part of the show. Magda reached down for the woman's hand to help her up. Fully embarrassed in front of all those people, the fallen woman swore at Magda, spit at her, and stomped off back into the crowd, which applauded her exit. Magda took a bow and finished her show.

All would have been well had the brawny woman not retreated to her favorite bar where, after numerous drinks, she had been convinced by the attendant barroom lawyers and self-appointed judges that she had a clear case of assault and inappropriate touching. A lawyer was recommended, and the fuss was started. What the assembled team of legal experts and the aggrieved woman, whose name was Candy, failed to consider was that there was a bleacher full of witnesses, most of whom did not see it her way. The case crumbled, Magda was exonerated, and Candy slunk back to her favorite watering hole.

"No, we ain't blaming you, Magda," continued Abbie, "we just need to be careful, that's all. That case cost us a lot of money in lawyer fees and it puts our reputation in question. Guilty or not, people's opinions are affected by such accusations and doubt almost invariably falls on the negative side. I know that some of you, over the years, have formed, er, friendships in the towns that we visit regularly. I'm not saying that you have to stop, just be discreet. Okay?"

Everyone murmured their assent, some more reluctantly than others. Only Zelda looked a little put out, probably because it was her sister who again had finally handled the whole episode.

• • • • •

All this came flashing back to the cross-eyed clown as he stealthily tried to get out of the motel room. It was one of those old-fashioned, one-storied motels with all the rooms set in a u-shape around the swimming pool. Just as the clown was about to step outside, he saw across the way, another door open. He quickly pulled back into the room, carefully pulled back an edge of the old, stiff and nicotine-stained curtain to get a better look at his fellow escapee. There was a light on in the room across the court, and the clown could plainly see the back-lit silhouette of two people kissing. Then one turned and hurriedly walked away as the other quickly shut the door. Their faces and bodies were in shadow, and with his bad eye, it was hard to tell who they were let alone what they were — two men, two women, or a woman and a man, but the one who was leaving was tall and their posture, as they quickly walked away, left little doubt in the clown's mind as to who that person was.

"Well, whaddaya know?" the clown almost spoke aloud as he slowly put the curtain back in place and tucked this new information into the hold-all of his mind for possible future use. After first seeing the light go out in the room across the way and checking that the departing silhouette had completely disappeared, he too silently slipped out into the cool morning darkness.

ERASMUS

Erasmus was the name bestowed upon him at birth. His father, a lay preacher, was a limited man, limited in just about every aspect — height, weight, hair, teeth, looks, education, intelligence, goodwill, the Christian Spirit, and most of all, self-awareness. He admired intellectuals, especially those of the Christian variety, hence the name Erasmus. His son, however, did not share his father's enthusiasm, especially regarding his choice of names. Even the teachers at school would sometimes mockingly comment about the name. When, at the age of six, his right eye started to wander on its own path, separate from the left, that was it for Erasmus. Not only did his name single him out, but now his eyes were betraying him. Everyone at school had a nickname, and the more popular you were, the cooler the nickname. Before his eye went bad, the kids would call him Izzie, and he hated that. He knew it was really short for Isobel, and what young boy wants a girl's name? He desperately tried to introduce Raz or The Raz as his name, to no avail. Then when his eye started wandering, he became "cocky eyes" or "cocky" for short. Even his father took to mocking him.

"Ifn you cain't look anyone straight in the eye, how're they gonna trust you, boy?"

It took Erasmus a while to figure out how to deal with this new setback, but in the space of a year he went from "Cocky," the awkward, withdrawn and clumsy boy, to the "The Raz," the school bad-ass. Not necessarily a bully, just a bad-tempered somebody that you didn't mess with. At first, he couldn't fight worth a shit. Because of his misaligned eyes, his depth perception was off, he couldn't connect with his punches, and he could be so easily blind-sided. With the will of the downtrodden, Erasmus leaned to adjust and how to fight in close quarters, mainly by watching fight scenes from kung-fu movies on YouTube. The other boys stayed clear of him; they no longer mocked him, at least to his face. It was his attitude that was now noticed not his name or his eyes. With a small scar from one of his earlier fights that gave him that edgy look, he wasn't bad looking, and some of the girls became attracted to him.

Things changed drastically for Erasmus when he graduated from school. The real world was a lot faster, tougher, and even more unkind. The bad-asses out there were bigger, badder, and stronger and knew a great deal more about street fighting than he did. The women, too, were bigger, badder, and stronger, not so easily won over by the bad-ass act. He was forever being slapped by women for looking at them inappropriately. His "bad" eye was not only off center from his "good" eye but also tended to look downwards. Women, unaware that Erasmus' brain had long ago learned to ignore the input from the "bad" eye, were disconcerted and then insulted by the direction of his wandering gaze. Outraged that he might be ogling their breasts or trying to look down their blouse, they'd slap him and walk away. Some men were excited by his one-eyed wanderings, which led to other misunderstandings and the inevitable violent reaction from Erasmus. Forming relationships for Erasmus was tough, to say the least.

None of the armed forces would take him because of his eyes, so he drifted around for a while looking for a suitable job for a bad-ass. There weren't that many openings for bad-asses even in the small West Texas town where he lived. One day, when the rodeo came to town, he was watching the whole show, noting the interactions between the different rodeo workers, their pecking order. Erasmus was impressed by the cool, hard way the cowboys, the bronc and bull riders, held themselves. They were the center of attention, and they were tough, nobody seemed to mess with them, and they attracted a certain type of woman. Somehow, he got to know one of these cowboys, who put him up on a horse. The horse, which wasn't strapped to buck, sensed Erasmus' nervousness and bucked in any case. Erasmus went flying, the first of many failed attempts to just sit on a horse. It was soon decided that Erasmus could no more ride a horse than he could look someone straight in the eye. The next day, the rodeo clown who'd been out drinking and drugging all night was gored by one of the bulls, and Erasmus got the job.

Again, that lack of depth perception came into play, but luck finally teamed up with Erasmus, and he escaped the worst of hoof and horn. The crowds, too, loved the extremely close calls and near misses, which added to the overall excitement of the show and, eventually, higher attendance. Erasmus became almost as well-known as some of the riders and was billed as, *The Cross-Eyed Clown*.

Erasmus wasn't too pleased with that particular name, even though they pitched it to him as a stage name, but he was getting a lot more recognition than he ever had before. People actually paid to see him and cheer him on. It was a moot point whether they came to admire his bravery—all the close calls—or to relish his stupidity and hope to see him caught by horse hoof or bull horn. Either way, Erasmus liked the attention. The rough and ready culture of the rodeo circuit allowed him to act out his bad-ass persona right until he started fighting with some of the customers. He had never learned how to deal with hecklers except with his fists, and beating up customers, especially in front of other customers, was bad for business, and eventually, Erasmus was fired from some of the best rodeo outfits.

Erasmus was on his way down when he met the midget, who was on his way up. The unlikely couple hit it off almost immediately and quickly developed a fast-paced and amusing act built around the clown's bad eye and the midget's size and speed. Everything went well for a while until one day the wrong customer yelled the wrong thing at the midget, which threw off his timing. The clown's quick thinking diverted the bull's horns at the very last second, saving the midget. Then the clown dove into the crowd to find the heckler, and he was fired again.

"The trouble with habits," the midget had said, "is that they are rarely recognized as such by the habitué."

"Whaddaya mean?" asked the cross-eyed clown distractedly, his main focus being on the crossword puzzle he was working.

"The answer is Euphrates," said the midget.

"I, what?" asked the clown still semi-absorbed in his puzzle.

"No, Euphrates; the river; is the answer to the clue, 'Waters of Baby-lon.' Now, put that down, and listen to me for a change. This is serious. You're running out of options. You've just been fired again for fighting. How many times has that happened? You've got a reputation, and no-one will hire you anymore," the midget continued.

"I know that," spat back the cross-eyed clown. "You don't have to keep rubbing it in."

"If you want to continue being a rodeo clown, if you want to be hired again, you've got to change, and the spark for change is self-awareness. You have the habit of fighting. You've done it for so long and so often, you don't even know you're doing it. The bad news is that fighting's be-come a conditioned response, a habit; the good news is that habits can be broken."

The midget looked at the expression on his friend's face and decided to stand up to better facilitate his escape should he accidentally pull the hair trigger that was the clown's temper.

The clown's one good eye glared at the midget.

"You my shrink, now?" was all he said.

"No, I'm just your friend. I can get us a job with this traveling show, but you've got to change. It's run by two sisters, and they won't tolerate any violence or any bullshit whatsoever."

The midget slowly resumed his seat next to the clown.

"What kind of show? I'm still gonna be a rodeo clown, ain't I?" The clown asked a little dubiously. "Are you going with me? You'll quit and stick with me?" The clown had never known this kind of loyalty before. He didn't trust it.

"Yes, I'll quit and come with you. I'm sick of these assholes. We work well together, and in spite of your violence, I kinda like you." The midget jumped to his feet again as the clown shot him another one-eyed glare.

"Like you as a friend," the midget hastened to add. "You stand up for me, we're a good team, and we share our l......" The midget was going to say "love," thought better of it, caught himself just in time, and quickly said, "Like. We both like crosswords."

The cross-eyed clown was silent for quite a while, and the midget knew him well enough to let him be. The midget was short in stature but not short on brains. He and the cross-eyed clown both had high I.Q.s not that they'd ever been measured. But their intellect set them a bit apart in the closed community of the rodeo circuit where differences always seemed to cause conflict and conflict invariably led to fighting.

Eventually, the clown looked up and said, "Okay, let's go and meet these friends of yours." Once they were in the pick-up truck, driving away, the clown asked, "You really think I can change?"

"Yup," said the midget.

"Hm," said the cross-eyed clown as he tapped his fingers on the steering wheel. "What's the name of this outfit we're going to see?"

"Honeycutt's Traveling Rodeo and Genuine Old Fashioned Medicine Show."

JOE THE INDIAN

No one really knew about Joe the Indian, and Joe the Indian liked it that way.

No one really knew Joe the Indian's real name, and Joe the Indian liked that, too. J.D. sometimes called him Joseph. But that wasn't his name, and Joe the Indian never corrected J.D. Everyone just called him Joe the Indian. Zelda certainly knew his name, from his Social Security card and for tax purposes, but getting her to give up information was like asking a priest to divulge secrets from the confessional. It would never happen.

Joe the Indian always used his Indian name, in the language of his people, even on official documents. He refused to use a white man's name. When Joe the Indian had first shown up, Zelda asked, "What do people call you?" after she had tried and failed to pronounce his Indian name.

"Indian Joe," replied Joe the Indian. He made a wry expression and shrugged.

Zelda laughed. "You know where that's from, don't you?" she asked.

"Yes ma'am," Joe replied. "Tom Sawyer. It was also the name of a famous Indian Scout. I think I'd rather just be plain old Joe."

Just then Abbie came into the trailer, and without thinking, Zelda said, "Gail, this is Joe the Indian. He's our new stock man."

Abbie stuck out her hand and said, "Howdy, Joe the Indian. People 'round here call me Abbie. Welcome aboard."

And that's how it started.

"You can use that desk over there," said Zelda indicating a wobbly looking old metal desk with an ancient, black plastic rotary dial phone half sunk in a sea of folders, invoices, and old, stained Styrofoam cups. "We'll get you a company cell phone. All the supplies and such are locked in the storage room at the back end of the trailer."

The sisters had bought an old construction trailer that had been used as an onsite office. They'd had it painted with the Show's logo; a large, colorful, copy of an old Wild West Show advertisement. It was almost psychedelic in design, the large red letters seemingly floating across the whole yellow background scene of horses, bulls, cowboys, Indians, and a bison, although their show didn't possess such an animal, yet. The logo/painting was Zelda's pride and joy. She had a friend who'd done it for free.

What was known about Joe the Indian?

That he was from Oklahoma. The state.

That he had been with Honeycutt's Traveling Rodeo and Genuine Old Fashioned Medicine Show longer than anyone else.

That Joe the Indian didn't like the cross-eyed clown from the git go. The clown thought Joe was scared of him because Joe wouldn't look him in the eye. Besides the fact that it was virtually impossible to look directly into both the clown's eyes at the same time, Joe the Indian wouldn't look into the clown's eyes because in his culture, it was rude to look anyone in the eyes. No, in his life around cowboys and rodeos, Joe had seen too many men like the cross-eyed clown. Violent men. Sudden men, his people had called them. Men quick to anger and violence.

"Give him a chance," pleaded the midget in a rare cordial moment between the two of them. "He's really making an effort to change."

Joe the Indian looked over at the clown, who was angrily tearing up a book of crossword puzzles in the shade. He looked back at the midget and said, "Seeing is believing, dwarf," and staggered off.

No one really knew if Joe the Indian had ever been a real drunk.

Everyone on the crew knew Joe the Indian just acted drunk, and if they didn't, they were soon put right, either by J.D. or Abbie herself. The cross-eyed clown had his doubts.

"That Indian's pulling a double con. He's faking being drunk, pretending he's sober, when he really is drunk in the first place," he'd explained to J.D. soon after he'd first joined the show. "I know Injuns, and they're a sneaky bunch of SOBs." The clown had had a few slugs of whiskey himself by then.

J.D. sniffed loudly close to the clown's mouth and said, "Smells like a pot's a-callin' a kettle black to me," and he walked off softly singing a song about rye whiskey.

"I know he's a real drunk," shouted the cross-eyed clown at J.D.'s back.

"Prove it," yelled J.D.

If the truth were known, the cross-eyed clown didn't "know injuns" at all. Thanks in part to the U.S. Cavalry and the Texas Rangers, there were no Indians in the small West Texas town where the clown grew up. He'd seen a few Indians during his travels with various rodeos, but not until Honeycutt's had he worked and lived side by side with an Indian. For a while, the cross-eyed clown went on a tear, going through Joe the Indian's garbage and once even sneaking into his camper trying to find bottles and evidence of him drinking. He found nothing and soon grew weary of the whole pursuit. Joe the Indian continued to avoid the clown as much as possible, which only increased the clown's belief in both the Indian's fear and in his subterfuge.

Joe the Indian pretty much avoided everyone and kept to himself. Where many of the crew shared trailers and RVs, Indian Joe had his own small RV. One of those camper tops loaded onto an old Chevy pickup truck. It was unexceptional. He had no Indian regalia stuck to it or hanging from it; no dream catchers in the windows, no miniature tom-toms hanging from the rearview mirror. He did not want to be noticed.

When he first started, both Zelda and Abbie wanted him to wear a big old war bonnet when the show was open and customers were around. Joe the Indian refused, point blank.

"Sitting Bull wore one for Buffalo Bill," Abbie tried to persuade Joe the Indian.

"I ain't a chief. Besides, look what they did to him," was all Joe would say and walked off.

ZELDA

"**S**he's a speed listener," said Joe the Indian.

"A what?" asked J.D.

"A speed listener," repeated Joe. "You know how some people speed read?"

J.D. nodded

"They skip over most of the words when they're reading, just to get at the gist of what is being communicated. Of course, it's mainly done on reports and such where everything is factual. You couldn't do it reading a novel though," continued Joe.

"Well, you could," interjected J.D. "But you'd lose half the worth, the sense, the subtlety, the art of the author."

"And that's exactly what she does, only when listening not reading. She only hears or acknowledges selective words, so she gets the drift of what's being said. Trouble is, nine times out of ten she gets the wrong drift, she misinterprets the meaning, hence the constant confusion." Joe the Indian stood up triumphantly and took a wobbly bow for his expert evaluation of Zelda's problem.

J.D. laughed, shook his head and said, "You're so full of shit, Joseph."

Joe the Indian looked crestfallen.

"Whaddaya mean, 'full of shit'? I'm serious."

"Speed listening, that's a good one, I'll give you that," said J.D., who was quickly trying to mend Joe's bruised feelings. "What I think is, Stoop is so tall, her head is in the clouds, and some words don't quite reach up to that altitude; the air is too thin to support their weight."

J.D. tried to keep a straight face for as long as possible, but it was only a couple of moments before they both doubled over laughing.

Strangely, they were both right about Zelda's hearing. She did have a form of selective hearing because her head was in the clouds. Zelda was a dreamer, a constant dreamer; her mind would not stop dreaming. Only the occasional word or two from a conversation would seep through the incessant barrage of thoughts, ideas, and fantasies that blitzed her mind. Abigail, with that telepathic, almost sixth sense, with which twins are supposedly endowed, was one of the few who could fully and completely communicate with her sister. Well, "fully" might be stretching it a bit, but they did manage to communicate with very few misunderstandings.

As a child, Zelda was fine; children were almost expected to be in a world of their own. As an adult, the world that her mind lived in was a far, far better place than the one in which her body existed, and this created problems both for her and for the other creatures with whom she was destined to coexist. Zelda's was a world of words and numbers, images and ideas, dreams and fantasies. These latter could swirl so fast and with such whirlpool intensity, they would drag her down into the vortex of oblivion, and Abbie would have to forcibly bring her back to reality.

Fortunately, Zelda had learned to recognize the impending onslaught of such episodes and had, purely by accident, discovered an antidote. A rather pleasant antidote, for her at least, and that antidote was an age-old remedy used throughout time by both men and women to cure numerous and sundry ailments. That magical antidote was sex. Plain old, simple sex, fornication, coitus, coupling, the conjoining of two human beings. Simply put, fucking stopped the brain barrage in Zelda's head.

26

The balance was restored between body and mind. For the duration of the act and for a day or so following, Zelda's mental torrent would cease until it slowly built back up again. Self-gratification was only partially and sporadically effective. The sex had to involve another person and that other person had to be male. No one really knew why. No one really knew, period; except for Abbie.

"You've got to be careful, Zell. What if someone sees you?" Abbie had met her coming back from the motel that morning. "You can't go threatening to dock people's pay for doing exactly the same thing as you."

"I am careful, Gail." Zelda liked to call her Gail. It was their special name. Everyone else called her Abbie. "Besides, who's going to see me at this hour of the day, except my nosy sister?"

"I dunno. I just don't want you to get caught in an embarrassing situation. You know what some of these guys are like, always looking for an edge and perhaps a pay-off." Abbie was putting on her boots and stamped her heel a little too hard, which startled Zelda.

"There's no need to get nasty about it. At least I have a sex life," snapped Zelda, and she stormed back to her sleeping berth on the bus. They had one of those large, custom-made buses that used to belong to an old female country singer.

Abbie took one step towards following her sister back and continuing the argument. Thought better of it. Stopped. Turned around, poured herself a cup of coffee, and went outside to sit under the awning that was pulled out from the side of the bus. That was when she saw the cross-eyed clown coming back from the same direction as the motel. The clown didn't seem to notice Abbie and slowly climbed into the beat-up old fifth-wheeler that he shared with the midget. For a horrified moment, Abbie imagined the cross-eyed clown and Zelda together in the motel room.

"Nah," she said out loud. She shook her head and went inside for another cup of coffee.

Zelda was sitting in the desk area already working on the books. She took care of all the books, the accounting, all the paperwork, the endless licensing as well as the creative aspects of all the advertising. She was happy to do it as it helped focus a small area of her battered brain. Abigail took care of the brawn aspects, not that she was a dummy. Not by any means. She was just good at dealing with both people and animals. Between the two of them, Abigail and Zelda, they had the perfect division of labor.

Abigail topped up her coffee mug and sat down opposite her sister.

"Listen, Zell. I wasn't checking up on you, and I don't mean to get on your case. I know what you do and why you have to do it. I wish there was something more I could do…" Abbie's voice trailed off as she ran out of things to say.

Zelda took her time finishing whatever she was doing before putting down her pen and looking at her sister.

It can't be her mind thing, 'cos she's just had her fix, so she must be pissed, thought Abbie.

Zelda reached for her glass of orange juice and took a sip. She didn't drink coffee. With the way her mind operated, caffeine was not a good idea. She was momentarily enjoying her sister's evident discomfort. Zelda's face assumed an expression she'd seen on models' faces; that vacant, self-absorbed look that people mistake for haughtiness. Then she relaxed her face and spoke.

"Sometimes I hate myself for the way I am. I hate that I have to find strangers to fuck."

Abbie reached across the table to take her sister's hand.

"Sometimes, when my mind is calm and the tempest is not raging, that old self-doubt monster comes crawling out. You just stepped on her tail, that's all," said Zelda with a sad look on her face. "Sometimes I wish I could find a husband, someone to fuck any time I needed to. But that would just become boring after a while, and he'd want sex when I didn't. I'm like you, Gail, I'm really not that interested in sex, and I'm happier by myself."

"Yeah, it's weird how we're both like that. As long as we have each other, we're happy to be alone."

Abbie made a face and twisted in her seat as if the paradox of that last statement made her uncomfortable.

"Yes, I know. I get it," said Zelda, smiling as she returned to her paperwork. She was way over her conversational limit, even with her sister.

ABIGAIL and ZELDA

James Stuart Turnbull, worked on the oil rigs that lay in the North Sea, off Scotland's east coast. He was an extrovert, both polite and pleasant, solidly built, and just under average height with a hard outer casing that sheltered a gentler soul within.

Heather Felicity MacCrainie was an introvert. She worked in a bookstore in Aberdeen, Scotland. She was tall, what some would call willowy, although why people are compared with trees is a puzzle. Perhaps the druids live on within us all. Heather was on the verge of being plain. It was that almost librarian look that saved her from being relegated to, in the opinion of some men, the not-worth-a-second-glance category. But James was different.

James liked books, he liked this particular bookstore, he really liked this particular bookstore clerk, and he really liked librarians. He gave Heather more than a second glance. Who can fathom the mechanics of attraction? Some would be horrified to think of the heart being compared with a cold insensitive machine. And the heart as the seat of love, where did that come from? We humans are peculiar thinkers. We can work out massively complicated theorems like quantum physics, the evolution of genetics, DNA, and even how to wade through the practical applications of government legislation. But if something cannot be explained or proven, then its cause is vaguely attributed to another random organ or entity. Religions are built on this, and so is the cult of the heart and the business of love.

They started dating; one thing led to another, and they were married. They say opposites attract, but there is no mention of compatibility in that statement. He had the standard librarian fantasies; she played along. Once married, the fantasies soon lost their appeal, and Heather grew tired of being someone she was not.

As is her wont, Mother Nature intervened at the most inappropriate time.

Heather was pregnant.

Twin girls were born, Abigail and Zelda.

James was happy and proud, although one baby boy would have been nice.

The double childbirth, however, did something to Heather's mind; a switch was flicked, a circuit was broken, or activated. Either way; over time her already fragile persona began to fracture. Even though James' work regularly kept him away, their marriage began to dissolve; the bonds of attraction began to fray. They struggled past the terrible twos with the twins, then James was laid off. The perfect time for a geographic cure.

James had a relative in Abilene, Texas: Uncle Rob. Like the pioneers of old, they would go there and start over. Not realizing that Abilene was some four hundred miles from the coast, James thought he could work on the oil rigs in the Gulf, and Heather could raise the twins on Uncle Rob's ranch.

James took to Texas as if he were born to be there. Heather took to Texas as if she had been consigned to hell. She hated the place, the heat, and the people. She was terrified of the Mexicans and repulsed by the brashness of the whites. Heather didn't wilt and wither away; she just caused everything and everyone around her to wilt and wither away. She became increasingly neurotic, which is a polite way of saying a royal pain in the ass. She was never happy, always fearful, constantly complaining, and ceaselessly critical.

James eventually found a job on the rigs, which kept him out of town on a regular basis. Finally, it was Uncle Rob who, stuck with the volatile and decidedly unfriendly Heather, delivered the ultimatum. Heather had to go. She was disrupting everyone's lives.

"Heaven knows what impact she's having on the kids," Uncle Rob had reasoned.

The divorce was a bitter affair with Heather pulling out all the stops. Somehow, she got Zelda to swear she would rather stay with her mother. Abigail, already showing signs of tomboyism, emphatically wanted to stay on the ranch.

The judge, also a twin, whose sister had died in a drive-by shooting at the age of ten, was very attuned to the special bond between twins. Unable, legally, to do anything about the girls being separated, she made it very plain that part of the divorce decree stipulated that visiting rights for the twins' sakes were adhered to by both parents.

"I don't care if one of you lives in Anchorage and the other in Key West, you will allow the twins their rightful time together," the judge had proclaimed with the slight hint of a catch in her throat.

Although James stayed in Abilene with Abigail, he was frequently away at work. She was basically raised by Uncle Rob, an aging and childless widower, who was the best thing to ever happen to Abigail. The uncle had a small horse ranch, and Abbie, as he called her, was given the freedom of it. She learned everything a good horse wrangler should learn — the three Rs: Riding, Roping, and Rifles. She was a free-ranger; not wild in the troubled sense of the word, but fiercely and very capably independent.

Heather, with Zelda in tow, moved to Maryland, where she had a sister who helped her get back on her feet, and then as soon as she could, pushed them both out on their own. Heather, as neurotic as ever, got a job working for the USPS, where she fit right in and applied for citizenship. Her neuroses were so firmly entrenched in her psyche and her incessant complaining, vocalized criticisms, fears, and smothering attachment for Zelda, drove the poor girl deep within herself. She retreated to the land, an island really, of thoughts and dreams and silence.

Zelda missed her sister. Her sister missed her. On the times the twins were together, they were almost inseparable. Abigail would try to get Zelda interested in horses, and guns, and ranch life, but Zelda was happy just to tag along. As long as she was with her sister, she felt safe and at peace. Abigail went once to Maryland, never to return. One time, when Zelda was visiting and didn't want to go back to Maryland, she and Abigail hid in a secret place so that no one could find them. They lasted for three days before the ranch hands finally tracked them down in a gulch, much to the relief of the local sheriff, who was being phone bombed hourly by Heather up in Maryland, who thought her daughters had been kidnapped by a Waco-type cult.

"There's no telling what those barbaric Texans will do. They're worse than the English," Heather would proclaim to her fellow postal workers, who were growing increasingly concerned about Heather's neurotic behavior, the term "going postal" being ever present in their fears.

When the twins turned sixteen their worlds turned upside down.

Heather was "retired" from the USPS on disability.

James was killed in an oil rig accident.

Uncle Rob took charge. He applied for, and won, custody of Abigail and Zelda. Heather was on so much medication, she was virtually a zombie. The insurance pay-off from James' accident assured that, if handled properly, the twins would be set for life. Uncle Rob made sure it was handled properly. Zelda moved to Abilene, and the twins finally felt complete again. Zelda, of course, was a bit strange, but she was quiet and fit right in. Uncle Rob started to teach both Abbie and Zelda how to run the ranch, his way, by the three B's: "Be fair. Be honest. Be aware." Rob liked things in threes. He would say it over and over again. Zelda learned how to do the books and all the necessary paperwork; Abigail happily took care of the rest.

This lasted for a couple of years before cancer took Uncle Rob, quite suddenly and devastatingly for the twins. He left the ranch to them, and they were on their own. Sad as they were at losing the one person who symbolized family and unconditional love to them, Abbie and Zelda still had each other. They were good at running the ranch. Zelda had the imagination to develop new ideas and projects; Abbie had the strength and knowhow to implement them, and thanks to their father and Uncle Rob, they had the means to carry them out.

After a few years, Abbie got restless, and if she got restless, it meant that Zelda got restless, too. It seemed like if one got an itch, the other would scratch it. Their ranch had been supplying horses to a few rodeo outfits; the twins were invited to attend some shows. Abbie started competing and to her surprise started winning, not only at riding but shooting as well. She became well-known as *Abilene Abbie*; Zelda was happy to just tag along. They started to travel more and found they liked the constant change of scenery and personnel. One of the Mexican ranch hands made an excellent and trustworthy manager to oversee the ranch while the twins were off rodeoing through the West.

One fateful week, the twins were in Oklahoma, and they happened upon Pawnee Bill's museum. Like Buffalo Bill, Pawnee Bill had run a traveling Wild West Show. Abbie and Zelda stood and looked at the all the pictures and posters in those bright primary colors. They read the stories. They were in awe of the scenes of horses and bison, cowboys and bulls, Indians and sharpshooters, and they fell in love. If you could have seen their faces, their eyes wide and almost tearful with excitement; looking first at the exhibits, then at each other, then back to the pictures. They didn't need words to communicate; each was moved in the same way, each thought the same thoughts, each loved the same idea. The seed was sown and from it had grown Honeycutt's Traveling Rodeo and Genuine Old Fashioned Medicine Show.

INTERLUDE

"Every profession has its own groupies," stated J.D.

"You reckon garbage men have groupies?" asked Joe the Indian.

"White trash," came back J.D. quick as a flash. They both tumbled about laughing.

J.D. and Joe the Indian were sitting in the shade on a couple of old, rusted beach chairs, smoking a joint. The two of them were safe, they thought, tucked out of sight by the livestock trailers where people rarely ventured. Mainly because of the stink and the flies.

"I wonder how much words weigh. I mean, if you could somehow pour all the words off the pages, out of a book, you know, just hold a book up by its spine and shake all them words out of it, how much would the book then weigh? Or, how much would that pile of words weigh?"

J.D. was stoned; capital S T O N E D; very stoned. Joe the Indian, who was not that far behind his friend in stonedness, just looked at J.D., trying to find the right words to fit in his mouth.

"What's a heavy word?" Joe the Indian finally found some words that just sort of dribbled out of his mouth, as if he were at the dentist's.

"Lugubrious, sounds heavy," mused J.D.

"What?" Those four letters seemed to take forever to come out.

"Lugubrious," said J.D. and sounded it out for Joe the Indian, "Loo - goo - bree - us."

"What's it mean?" asked Joe in a rare moment of clarity.

"I can't remember," mumbled J.D.

"Loo-goo-br…whatever, means, 'I can't remember'?" Big words and long tokes combined generally create confusion. Joe the Indian was genuinely confused.

"No. I can't remember what the word lugubrious means, dumbass," chuckled J.D.

"Hm. Must have something to do with oiling; needing oil. Like, those squeaky wheels are sounding loo - goo - bree - us to me." Joe the Indian was getting into it now.

"Then it would be lubri something," said J.D.

Joe the Indian started singing, "Loo - bree - goo - bree - dee, loo - bree - goo - bree - da..." J.D. joined in before they both dissolved into fits of giggles.

Just then, Zelda came around the back of one of the trailers. The guys jumped like two school kids caught smoking, or worse; Indian Joe straightened his shirt and then, inexplicably, his pants, which were in no need of it. J.D. looked around frantically for some place to hide the joint; well, he would have looked frantic if he hadn't been so stoned. He gave up and, with a brave grimace, stuck it in his mouth, the lit end briefly burning his tongue before his saliva extinguished it. Then, he, too, straightened his clothing, assumed what he believed to be an innocent expression, and calmly looked at Zelda.

Having remained silent and managing to keep a straight face for the duration of this Cheech and Chong act, Zelda finally laughed out loud. The two stoners looked at each other, their suppressed giggles finally bursting to the surface and joined Zelda in the laugh fest, the sodden joint falling in bits out of J.D.'s mouth. Zelda, being the un-stoned one, was the first to stop laughing.

"Keep it cool and out of sight, is all I ask guys," said Zelda in her dreamy like voice.

"Yes, ma'am," said J.D. as he reached into his shirt pocket, pulled out another joint and with his hand extended towards Zelda said, "You want some, Zelda?"

Joe the Indian gave him a hard nudge in the ribs for that one.

"No thanks, J.D.," replied Zelda, "I don't need it." And she walked away.

"Huh?" said J.D. and Joe the Indian simultaneously. They really were becoming a comedic duo.

"What's she mean by that?" mused Joe the Indian.

J.D. said, "You got me."

"Babe," added Joe the Indian almost automatically and they both started laughing again.

"Hey, we ought to work this into the show," said J.D. enthusiastically.

"Not with me, you're not," stated Joe the Indian emphatically.

They argued back and forth for a while, but Joe the Indian would not budge from his non-involvement stance, no matter how hard J.D. wheedled and pleaded.

"I'll not be no cigar store Indian," mumbled Joe sulkily.

The more J.D. talked and thought about it, the more he liked the idea. If Joe the Indian wouldn't do it, and J.D. respected his reasons for not doing it, he'd have to find somebody else. A female would be good, but she'd have to be special—strong, but not overpowering, fairly good looking and/or presentable, and preferably a musician. He could use another musician, with a good singing voice, too, and one who could do good harmonies to boot.

Now J.D. was getting really excited about the whole idea. He bid farewell to his friend who was not too sad to see him go as he had his own chores to do. J.D. rushed back to his own bus to write out his ideas before they disappeared into the mists of stoned lethargy. He lay down on the bed and promptly fell fast asleep.

J.D.

"**S**o, what can we do for you, Mr. Williams?" asked Abbie in her best business-like voice. Zelda caught the cold, hard inflection of Abbie's tone and gave her sister a quick, puzzled look. They were sitting in the office trailer, Abbie, Zelda, and J.D.

"Well, I'd like to join your show, and please call me J.D.," he said pleasantly.

"In what capacity do you wish to join our show, Mr. Williams? You don't look like a wrangler or a cowboy, and you don't look strong enough to carry a bale of hay, never mind shovel shit for a day," Abbie continued with her stony attitude.

Her disdainful stance was making J.D. a little uncomfortable.

"I've watched your show for the past two nights, and I think I can add some aspects to the entertainment side that might pick it up a notch or two."

J.D. nervously fidgeted in his seat, while Miss Abbie just looked straight at him.

Why doesn't the other sister speak? wondered J.D. She just looked spaced out to him. Under the double scrutiny of bad cop, space cop, J.D. laughed nervously.

"Are you stoned, Mr. Williams? Because if you…"

"Gail," Zelda finally spoke, interrupting her sister with a hand gesture. Then she looked at J.D. and asked, "Would you be kind enough to wait outside, J.D.? My sister and I have some matters to discuss."

If there is a way to stand up grumpily, J.D. managed to find it, and he shut the door none too gently on his way out.

"Spoiled little brat," spat Abbie as the door closed behind J.D.

"What the hell's got into you, Gail? You're treating the poor man like he's some high school kid; asking if he's stoned."

"Well, his eyes are all red, and he's nervous as a polecat in a perfume parlor," replied Abbie.

"Of course he's nervous with you giving him the third degree. You know who he is, don't you? Who his parents are?" Zelda continued. "His mother is an internationally famous classical musician, and his dad is Joe Williams, and everybody knows who Joe Williams is."

"Yeah, yeah, I know, I know. The kid was a prodigy playing Mozart on the piano at four years old and playing God knows what by the time he was ten. He's rich as hell, but according to the papers, since he dropped out of Julliard, he ain't done much of anything. He's just bummed around living off mummy and daddy. You know I've got very little time for rich kids, Zell." Abbie, who could never sit still for very long, got up and stomped around the cramped space.

"If I didn't know any better, I'd figure that you fancied him," said Zelda with a smile.

"What?" retorted Abbie.

"The way you're treating him, an' all," Zelda just had to add. "Look, let's just see what he has to say. Maybe we can use him. Old Marty's just drunk all the time since his main squeeze dumped him back in Arizona. The band is sounding pretty bad these days."

Abbie paced around some more, weighing the pros and cons of having a "name" associated with the show. More people equals more money, but what kind of people? Certainly not rodeo people. It could turn 'round and bite them in the ass if those people just came to poke fun.

"I don't know, Zell," she finally said.

"Look," said Zelda rifling through some papers on the desk, "he's left his notes about his ideas. Let's have a look through them and see what we think."

Meanwhile, outside, J.D. was doing his own pacing back and forth. He was upset. He'd never been treated this way before. Most people knew who and what he was and would fall over themselves to have him work with them. Who did this little cowgirl think she was? The irony was that the only thing that J.D. had ever had to fight for was his freedom, his independence. Now he was offering to give that up, and it wasn't being accepted. All his life he'd been pushed and praised, paraded, pampered, and then prodded into trying even harder. By the time he got to Julliard, he was sick of being the puppet. He knew music theory and application backwards and standing on his head, he was sick of it, he wanted to escape the bonds of form and technique. Diversity was what excited him; specialization dulled him. Not wanting to focus on just one or two instruments and the restrictions of the classical form, J.D. angrily burst out of the confines of Julliard. His parents were irate, hurt, bewildered, and worried, but they were supportive, at least monetarily, although J.D. tried to insist on paying his own way. He bummed around the San Francisco Bay area playing with a couple of bands, but he found them just as constricting as Julliard.

A long time ago, J.D. had tired of the rich Marin County residents and their lifestyle. The constant media attention focused on his parents, and thus deflected onto him, made him seek his friendships elsewhere. He used to like to hang out in the upper Central Valley where the people were more basic, agricultural. Sure, they were more rightwing, but he could overlook the latter easier than he could the trendy, lip-service liberalism of his affluent friends and neighbors in Marin County.

One day, he was stoned and sitting in the parking lot of an *am-pm* convenience store in Lodi; having no deep thoughts, just chilling. He

43

looked up and saw a crow land a few feet away, pecking at something on the ground. Then the bird starting walking across the lot. J.D. watched the crow; did a double take. He looked, blinked his eyes, and looked again; the crow was limping, favoring its right leg. J.D. had never seen a crow limp before. Hell, he'd never seen any bird limp before. Mesmerized, he followed the lame crow's progress across the lot until a car pulled in, and the crow flew off. Following the flight of the crow, J.D. looked up and his eyes fixed upon an eye-catching, almost psychedelic poster for Honeycutt's *Traveling Rodeo and Genuine Old Fashioned Medicine Show*. Not wanting to ignore such an auspicious invitation, J.D. decided to go check out the show. He'd never been to a rodeo before.

He was thinking of the crow when the trailer door opened, and Zelda invited him back in.

"Sorry about that, J.D., but my sister and I had to make sure we were on the same page," explained Zelda with what she hoped was an encouraging smile.

J.D. returned the smile with a curt one of his own, nodded at Abbie, who nodded back, and then sat down at the gestured invitation.

"You have a history, Mr...er...J.D.." began Abbie.

"So do you," shot back J.D.

Abbie nodded with a rueful smile.

"Fame is not only fickle, but too often it's misunderstood. There are those who don't have it and want it, and those that have it and don't want it." Abbie paused and then started again. "I ain't a one to beat about the bush, so I'm gonna to lay my cards right out on the table. We may seem like a freaky little two-bit show to the likes of you, but we believe in what we do and are sincere in that belief. We give it our all, and we have fun doing it. Rodeoing is dangerous and we only employ professionals. We can't have young kids with stars in their eyes wanting to run away and join the circus. The people who work here are hard core; they certainly ain't the mothering type, and neither am I or my sister."

Now Zelda the space cop jumped in, "J.D., we took the liberty of looking through your notes about the musical aspects of our show. You left them here on the table."

J.D. just shrugged. What else could he do?

"We like some of your ideas, and we'd like to discuss them further with you," bad cop Abbie jumped back in. "Marty, our current musical director whom you refer to in your notes as 'a nursing home conductor' is about to retire, and we could use a replacement."

Zelda nodded with one of her enthusiastic, spacey smiles.

"I have one major concern, though," and quite a few minor ones, Abbie didn't add. "And, that is your name. Not the name itself, but the fame of the name, if you will."

"May I interrupt you before you go any further?" J.D. jumped in. I have given this a lot of thought. Personally, I don't want my name used. For reasons that may or may not be obvious, I'd rather be anonymous. Not that I would be ashamed to be associated with your show or rodeo, far from it, I'm actually excited. No, I'm tired of being known, of being a name." Here J.D. held his fingers up like quotation marks. "Also, I'm not sure that you would want the type of people that my name would attract attending your shows."

Zelda and Abbie looked at each other and smiled. "It seems like all our pages are beginning to be bound together," affirmed Zelda.

"I am just curious, though, as to how and why you picked our show. Why are we the ones to be favored with your talents, Mr. Williams?" Abbie asked, returning to her serious demeanor, but with a slight smile standing beside the question mark.

That small smile did more to relax J.D. than smoking a huge spliff would.

"A crow," was his answer.

"A crow?" asked Zelda and Abbie in twinly unison.

J.D. went on to tell the story of the crow, which later over time, developed into one of his favorite stories. He told the twins of his need for diversity, and originality, and freedom, and started to tell the twins about one of the amusing stunts he'd pulled back in high school, but one look at Abbie's still thawing expression made him quickly change his mind. They went on to discuss some of J.D.'s ideas for the show until Abbie grew visibly bored.

"There's one more thing you should know, J.D., before you make your final decision." Abbie, tired of sitting, had started pacing again, and J.D. did his best to follow her with his head. "We don't have many rules, can't abide them myself, but we have to have some, and Zelda will go over those with you. We're like a family here; dysfunctional maybe, like most families but a family nonetheless. We like our privacy, both public and personal. We have one unwritten rule, and that is the most important rule; we don't ask personal questions. When I say 'we,' I mean everybody, not just my sister and I. Privacy is expected and respected. Our motto is: 'Ask No Questions.' Follow that rule, and you'll be accepted into this family a lot faster."

THE MIDGET

"What the hell're you doin' sneakin' 'round at this hour?" asked the midget, grumpily. It was close to four AM, and his crooked grin was not in evidence at this hour.

"None of your goddamn business," snarled the clown.

"It is my business when you wake me up in the middle of the night, banging 'round, makin' coffee and stuff. And, this is about the fifth night in a row. It's getting as old as this coffee."

The midget spat out the dregs from his mug and went to make a fresh pot.

"You can't be spying on Joe the Indian again. He's never up at this hour."

"It ain't him," conceded the clown, "it's someone else."

"Well who, for God's sake. Just tell me. Perhaps I can help," suggested the midget.

Neither of them spoke for a while. The cross-eyed clown was weighing his confessional options, while the midget busied himself with fixing fresh mugs of coffee for them both.

There was more than a little paranoia in Erasmus' make-up. Long ago he'd figured out that if he couldn't beat people into submission the next best thing was to find the dirt. Everybody had dirt; something they were ashamed of, something they wanted kept a secret. Hell, he had a whole suitcase full of shit that he didn't want people to know about. Trouble was, digging for the dirt took time and effort and he was impatient and lazy. He'd easily and quickly found the dirt on the midget because they lived together in the trailer, and the midget was amazingly trusting, at least with Erasmus.

One weekend when the show was idle, the midget had gone off for a few days to spend time with some relatives. Erasmus got into the midget's room; hell, he had the keys, it was his trailer after all. He rifled, carefully he thought, through all the midget's stuff and found his personal papers. *Idiot should have put 'em in a lock box*, he thought to himself as a justification for his sneakiness. What he found, blew his mind. The midget's name was Juan Carlos Garcia, and he was Mexican. Erasmus just sat there, dumbfounded. Of all the things to find; his buddy, his roommate, the closest thing to a friend he'd ever had, probably ever would have, was a goddamned Mexican. Funny, he didn't look like one, he didn't sound like one either, and Erasmus never saw him eating beans and tacos and stuff or heard him listening to all that music with accordions wheezing and trumpets blaring.

Erasmus thought about his dilemma the whole weekend. What should he do with this new information? There were two lines of thought. First, the personal: could he continue to bunk with a Mexican? It would make them a Tex-Mex couple. Secondly, what kind of leverage could he gain with this new information? At the last moment, just as the midget was walking back through the door, Erasmus discovered that he was glad to see him; he had actually missed the midget being around. Erasmus decided to keep his discovery to himself; he could live with this particular Mexican. He even admired the midget for being able to keep this colossal secret for so long, when Erasmus himself could barely keep his own name a secret for more than a day or so. He'd told it to the midget on the third night they'd met.

"It's Stoop," the cross-eyed clown finally blurted out.

"Zelda?" asked the midget, incredulous.

48

"Yeah," affirmed the cross-eyed clown and proceeded to tell the midget about the night at the motel.

"Well, you can't blame a girl for wanting a bit of romance," the midget argued. He liked Stoop and perhaps because he was at the other end of the height spread, he sympathized with her; felt a bit sorry for her.

"Yeah but, who was she with? Was it another woman?" retorted the cross-eyed clown.

"So what if it was a woman she was with; who cares? It's the twenty-first century, and this is a free country," the midget threw back.

The cross-eyed clown was getting riled. *You should know*, he almost said, to his secret Mexican friend.

"Well, she shouldn't be doing that sort of thing when she's threatened to dock our wages for us doing it ourselves," grumbled the clown.

"No, but it's been my experience that he, or she in this case, who makes the rules invariably breaks the rules," reasoned the midget. "Why's it so important to you in any case?"

By now the cross-eyed clown was getting visibly agitated with his roommate for disagreeing with him.

"Knowledge is power. You'd be amazed at the things I know about people around here." He was on the verge of blurting out that he knew the midget's secret when the midget stole his thunder.

"I know you know about me; my real name and everything. I know you went through my stuff when I was away."

The midget backed up and out of range of potentially swinging fists.

The cross-eyed clown looked as though someone had kicked him in the nether regions. He was at a loss for both words and breath.

"How?" was all he managed to squeeze out of his vocal cords.

"You weren't very careful tidying up after you'd rifled through my things," the midget said simply and without rancor. "At first, I was pissed at you invading my privacy, but then I kind of expected it. If you work with snakes, chances are you're going to get bit."

The clown abruptly stood up and made to lash out at the little guy in front of him.

The midget, surprisingly, held his ground and smiled.

"Look, what you found out about me, that I'm Mexican, is no big deal. I'm legal; I have a green card. Stoop knows. I just don't like to advertise the fact that's all. Some people like to pick on Mexicans, especially little ones like me."

Erasmus sat back down, amazed at how calm the midget was.

"Look let's forget about me and what you did. Let's forget about Zelda. Leave the poor woman alone. I thought you were going to change."

"That was fighting," grumbled the cross-eyed clown.

"Same thing really, only worse," said the midget. "Physical bruises heal a lot faster than emotional ones. Whaddya say we drop the whole thing? You need to get some sleep, an' we got a show this afternoon. You need to have your wits about you."

JASPER

The announcer said, "And now, riding Jasper, is a newcomer to our great little rodeo, all the way from Spokane Washington, Travis Rawlins. Please give him a big welcome now."

Spoke and the bull, Jasper, came crashing and bucking out of the chute. Jasper, a cross between a Brahman and a Texas longhorn, was old and mean; a bad-ass. What, in rodeo parlance, they call a "honker." He was really giving Spoke a hard ride and finally bucked him off after only four seconds. Spoke fell to the side but became hung up in the riggin' and couldn't get free.

The cross-eyed clown, as any good bullfighter would, raced to help get Spoke free from the bull. The midget ran to the front of the bull to distract Jasper from hooking the other two with his horns. It was taking the clown longer than usual to free up Spoke. Just as he was reaching for a knife to cut the rope, he heard a God-awful racket.

Magda, the East European acrobat who has a thing for Spoke, had been watching from the stands. When she saw Spoke get hung up and dragged like a doll by the bull, she screamed and came running into the ring.

Higher up in the stands, the announcer saw her and over the PA said, "Magda stop. Stay where you are. Don't move. You'll only make things worse."

Magda, used to obeying orders barked by totalitarian officials, stopped where she was but continued screaming at the top of her lungs in a very high register. She screamed out words in her East European language that no one understood, least of all Jasper the bull. Magda continued to leap up and down, frantically waving her arms above her head. Jasper finally turned his attention to her, especially as she was wearing a bright red cape, part of her performance costume.

Jasper suddenly turned, causing the cross-eyed clown to drop the knife.

Jasper charged at Magda—the sudden movement jolted free whatever had Spoke trapped. Spoke and the clown fell in a tangled heap on the ground which, from high up in the stands, looked like a huge pile of dung left by the bull.

Free of the extra weight, Jasper charged even faster towards Magda, who was finally beginning to sense that something might be wrong.

The midget, seeing what had happened, raced to save Magda from being freight-trained. At the very last second, the midget was able to swing Magda out of the direct path of the charging bull, whose horns missed her throbbing jugular by a matter of centimeters.

By now, other cowboys and roustabouts were leaping into the arena, some rushing to help Spoke and the clown, others to protect Magda and the midget, who had also both fallen to the ground.

Magda had finally and thankfully quit her incessant caterwauling.

Abbie, who had been taking care of some business at the other side of the show grounds, heard all the commotion. Instinctively knowing that something had gone wrong, she rushed back towards the arena, grabbing her Winchester and the bull whip on her way.

By now, Jasper was fully enraged, he was stamping the ground and snorting, snot flying to the left and right, looking for the next target. It'd been so long since he'd had this much fun.

As Abbie ran towards the arena, she takes in the scene, the two groups of people and the bull. She could tell, just by looking at Jasper, that the bull wanted blood. The other cowboys were having no success in trying to steer Jasper towards the chutes and the paddock. The bull had them scared, and he knew it. Abbie climbed through the fence and cracked her whip, getting the bull's attention.

By now they were both on the far side of the arena, well away from the barricades and barrels—there was no protection; nowhere to hide.

Jasper focused on Abbie, watching her. Jasper had been around for a while and had learned a thing or two about how humans move and react. You could say, this was not his first rodeo. He started to charge.

Abbie raised the rifle to her eyes; she hesitated; she felt sorry for Jasper, understanding his behavior and wished she'd brought the dart gun. She hated killing animals; they couldn't afford to buy another bull. All this flashed through her mind as the bull was rapidly thundering closer.

She pulled the trigger.

Just as she pulled the trigger, the canny old bull set her up, turning slightly. The bullet hit him in the shoulder; he was only wounded, not disabled, and definitely not stopped.

He was just about on top of Abbie before she could get off another shot. At the last second, Jasper ducked off, turning his head again, and he caught Abigail full in the stomach with his horn and swung his massive head from side to side.

Abbie flew into the air and landed, seemingly lifeless, in a pile on the ground.

Jasper turned a few yards away, stops, stamped his front legs, snorted, lowered his head, and prepared to come at Abbie again for the coup de grace.

An eerie, "No," cut through the air.

"No," screamed Zelda again. Everybody was frozen in place as she leapt over the fence.

Jasper ignored her.

Zelda, cool as anything, picked up Abbie's rifle and began firing at the bull.

Jasper turned in her direction and began to charge at Zelda.

Her first shot missed.

Jasper kept coming.

The second shot hit him right where it was supposed to: squarely on the forehead.

Jasper kept coming.

Zelda kept firing.

Jasper's front knees finally buckled, and he came crashing down about a yard or so in front of Zelda.

Just as he was falling, Zelda got off another shot. The bullet ricocheted off one of Jasper's horns and flew off towards the center of the ring where the other cowboys and crew had managed to untangle Spoke and the cross-eyed clown. Spoke was in bad shape, but they were able to move him off the clown who, although battered and bruised, was not seriously injured. The cross-eyed clown finally stood up, looked over to where the bull was just beginning to fall at Zelda's feet. He heard the crack of the rifle, and that last deflected bullet hit him right between the eyes.

A stunned silence finally descended over Honeycutt's Traveling Rodeo and Genuine Old Fashioned Medicine Show.

Acknowledgements:

Phew, there are so many people to thank that this section could be longer than the story itself.

To all my friends who I used as sounding boards, you know who you are, and I thank you deeply. It was your positive attitudes that spurred me onwards. There are some whose help I sought and who gave freely of their time, sharing their experiences and valuable knowledge with me. Ellen Callahan, published author, is one such person. Although we have never met, she has willingly provided me with much valuable knowledge about writing and publishing through emails and phone calls. Buy her books; you won't be disappointed. Another such person is Steve Piscitelli, educator, writer, teacher, and friend. Ever since we first met, Steve has reached out the hand of friendship, offering advice when asked and suggesting possible directions.

I would be remiss if I did not mention Peter Bonta, accomplished friend, musician, sailor, and brother from a different mother. We have known each other a long time. His assistance and encouragement in all matters has sustained me immensely over the years. And then there is a group of men in Atlantic Beach, Florida, who have elevated the act of friendship to soaring new heights.

My wife, Mary, bore the brunt of the creative process, patiently listening to my thoughts and pointing out discrepancies and downright bad ideas. My lover and companion, she makes this journey so rewarding and enjoyable.

CPSIA information can be obtained
at www.ICGtesting.com
Printed in the USA
LVHW081143060520
655107LV00023B/3682